Maeve & Cora,

Hope you will always
have great friends
and be each other's
best friends!

Nanjin Mindy U

Published by Atmosphere Press

atmospherepress.com

Nami's New Friend

Written by Mandy Namjou Yom

Illustrations by Joanne Wong

atmosphere press

I dedicate this book to my parents, who left everything and everyone they knew and worked tirelessly to give me a better life.

Nami was bursting with wonder and excitement.
Her parents had told her amazing stories about
life in America.

Nami wondered if she would make new friends like the ones she was leaving behind in Korea.

Finally, the plane began to come down slowly, closer to the ground.

Nami stared at the glittery snow covering the land.

She had never seen snow so white.

Nami walked through the long airport hallway with her eyes wide open.

Soon she found herself in the middle of the airport lobby. She saw bright neon signs that she could not read and lots of restaurants with yummy smelling food.

Her dad grabbed their bags and led the family outside where her grandparents were waiting. She ran and hugged them before she got into the car.

When the car stopped in front of a red brick house, Nami smiled. She was home.

Nami fell asleep right away in her new bed,
in her new room, in her new home, in a new land.

Nami felt excited and nervous about her first day of school in America.

She sat on the bus wondering...

Will the kids want to play with me?

Will they want to be my friend?

Will they talk to me?

Nami's new teacher, Mrs. Kline, waved Nami up to the front of the class and introduced her. Nami didn't understand what Mrs. Kline was saying, but the way she kept smiling comforted her.

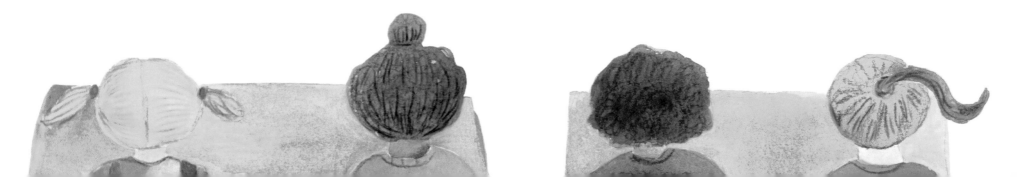

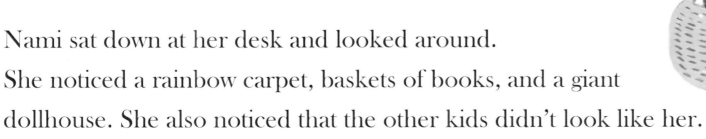

Nami sat down at her desk and looked around.
She noticed a rainbow carpet, baskets of books, and a giant
dollhouse. She also noticed that the other kids didn't look like her.

During lunch, Nami noticed that the food she brought was not like the other kids'. They had fluffy white bread with purple goo inside, while she had little balls of rice rolled up in seaweed.

At recess, Nami swung back and forth slowly on a swing. The kids on the swings beside her were talking and laughing. She wanted to join in, but she couldn't understand what they were saying.

Her eyes began to fill with tears as she wondered if she would ever get used to all these new things and make any friends.

When Nami saw her classmates lining up, she quickly ran to join them.

When Nami walked into the classroom, she saw a large piece of white paper, paint and brushes on all the desks.

Mrs. Kline gave instructions to the class. When she saw the other kids start to paint, Nami did, too.

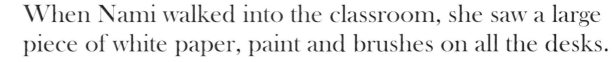

As Nami was painting the last purple petal, she heard her teacher's voice. The students started to put away their supplies. Nami did the same.

Mrs. Kline called out the students' names one at a time.
The kids took turns holding up their paintings.

Mrs. Kline called Nami's name. She held up her painting.
Suddenly, there was a loud giggle from the back of the classroom.

When Nami turned, she saw the girl who giggled. The girl held up her own painting, and Nami smiled. They had painted the same picture.

Nami sat back down feeling happy that she and the other girl had come up with the same idea.
She started looking around the classroom again.

ACHOOOO!

There was a girl sitting in the front row with pigtails just like hers. There was a boy to her left who had the same water bottle. Then, Nami heard another student in the back of the class sneeze, and it sounded like her sneeze! She smiled thinking how funny that was.

As everyone was getting ready to go home,
Nami thought maybe she just might get used
to this new school after all.

When Nami walked onto the bus, she heard someone call her name.

It was the girl who had painted the same picture!

Nami made her way to where the girl was sitting. The girl patted the empty spot next to her. She had saved Nami a seat!

The girl pointed to herself and said, "Sarah."

Nami pointed back and said, "Sarah."

Nami and Sarah looked out the window and made silly faces at the cars passing by. They giggled all through the bus ride home.

The bus stopped in front of Nami's new house. She waved to her new friend
Sarah and got off the bus.

Nami felt happy. Even though she had a lot to learn
about her new school, in her new life, in a new country,
she was excited she had found a new friend.

About the Author

Mandy Namjou Yom immigrated to the states from Seoul, South Korea when she was eight years old. She did not know how to speak a word of English at the time, and she ventured into her new world with mixed emotions not knowing how things would turn out. Things fortunately turned out well and she has come full circle. Mandy Namjou Yom has been working as a Kindergarten teacher for English Learners for the past 22 years in Illinois. She wrote this book to share her real-life experiences of what it was like being an immigrant child starting school for the first time in America. And to also show the language of friendship goes beyond spoken words and connections can be built in various ways.

About the Illustrator

Joanne Wong is a British born Chinese picture book illustrator and writer. She grew up in the suburbs of the UK and is a daughter of immigrant Hong Kong Chinese parents. The story of Nami and trying to 'fit-in' at school resonated deeply with her.

Joanne has always loved picture books, especially creating her own illustrations. She received a Master of Arts in Illustration from the University of Arts London at Camberwell College. Joanne currently lives in the sub-tropical countryside of Hong Kong with her family.

To see more of her work, go to www.joannewong

About Atmosphere Press

Atmosphere Press is an independent, full-service publisher for excellent books in all genres and for all audiences. Learn more about what we do at atmospherepress.com.

We encourage you to check out some of Atmosphere's latest releases, which are available at Amazon.com and via order from your local bookstore:

You are the Moon, a picture book by Shana Rachel Diot
Onionhead, a picture book by Gary Ziskovsky
Odo and the Stranger, a picture book by Mark Johnson
Jack and the Lean Stalk, a picture book by Raven Howell
Brave Little Donkey, a picture book by Rachel L. Pieper
Buried Treasure: A Cool Kids Adventure, a picture book by Anne Krebbs
Young Yogi and the Mind Monsters, an illustrated retelling of Patanjali by Sonja Radvila
The Magpie and The Turtle, a picture book by Timothy Yeahquo
The Alligator Wrestler: A Girls Can Do Anything Book, *children's* fiction by Carmen Petro
My WILD First Day of School, a picture book by Dennis Mathew
The Sky Belongs to the Dreamers, a picture book by J.P. Hostetler
I Will Love You Forever and Always, a picture book by Sarah Thomas Mariano
Shooting Stars: A Girls Can Do Anything Book, children's fiction by Carmen Petro
Oscar the Loveable Seagull, a picture book by Mark Johnson
Carpenters and Catapults: A Girls Can Do Anything Book, children's fiction by Carmen Petro
Gone Fishing: A Girls Can Do Anything Book, children's fiction by Carmen Petro
Bello the Cello, a picture book by Dennis Mathew
That Scarlett Bacon, a picture book by Mark Johnson
Makani and the Tiki Mikis, a picture book by Kosta Gregory

CPSIA information can be obtained
at www.ICGtesting.com
Printed in the USA
LVRC090014081021
699748LV00002B/7

9 781639 880409